Basil of Bywater Hollow

Basil of
Bywater Hollow

By Jill Baker

Illustrated by
Lynn Bywaters Ferris

Henry Holt and Company · *New York*

Limited edition prints and greeting cards
featuring the work of Lynn Bywaters Ferris are available from
Sunrise Publications, Bloomington, Indiana.

Copyright © 1987 by Sunrise Publications, Inc.
All rights reserved, including the right to reproduce
this book or portions thereof in any form.
Published by Henry Holt and Company, Inc.
521 Fifth Avenue, New York, New York 10175.
Distributed in Canada by Fitzhenry & Whiteside Limited,
195 Allstate Parkway, Markham, Ontario L3R 4T8.

Library of Congress Cataloging in Publication Data
Baker, Jill.
Basil of Bywater Hollow.
Summary: Basil thinks of himself as nothing but a
big, clumsy bear, until disaster strikes the fair and
his actions save the day.
[1. Bears—Fiction.   2. Fairs—Fiction.   3. Self-
perception—Fiction]   I. Ferris, Lynn, ill.   II. Title.
PZ7.B17425Bas   1986   [E]   85-24701
ISBN 0-8050-0268-5

First Edition

Printed in Italy
1   3   5   7   9   10   8   6   4   2

ISBN 0-8050-0268-5

For Rick   L.B.F.

With love to Mandy and Skip   J.B.

It was a beautiful morning in Bywater Hollow. Butterflies fluttered in the warm air, and bees darted among the fragrant flowers. In the raspberry patch, bluebirds swooped down to steal ripe berries from the bushes. Basil the bear watched all of this as he picked berries for his famous raspberry tarts.

"This is perfect weather for the summer fair!" he said to himself.

That afternoon the fair would open with rides like the merry-go-round and the Ferris wheel, and there would be a concert and, most important, a pie-eating contest! Basil licked his lips as he thought about big, juicy pies of every flavor lined up in rows before him. Then he realized that it was getting late. Surely Lily Underwood, owner of the Underwood Hotel where Basil was pastry chef, would be wondering where he was.

As he bent over to pick up his basket full of berries, his pants caught on the thorns of a raspberry bush. He pulled and he tugged, but the thorns held tight. He tried once more and heard the cloth rip as he freed himself. *I'll have to sew up that hole before this evening*, he thought. Then, with his basket in his paws, he lumbered off toward the Underwood Hotel.

The hotel restaurant was buzzing with activity as waiters and waitresses rushed in and out of the kitchen carrying large trays of hot biscuits, eggs, and tea.

"Hello, Lily!" said Basil as he opened the swinging doors. "Sorry I'm late. I was down at the berry patch, and I had a little accident."

Lily crossed her arms and tapped her foot.

"Basil, we have so many guests in for the fair today! I could have used your help with breakfast this morning. Well, thank goodness you're here. Be sure to make lots of your raspberry tarts."

"You can count on me, Lily," said Basil. "Here, taste one of these berries. That will cheer you up!!"

Just then a waiter pushed open the swinging door between the dining room and the kitchen and sent Basil and his berries flying. He landed on the floor with a loud THUMP. Red raspberries were strewn all over the kitchen floor.

"Looks like our guests will be eating leftover cookies for dessert," Lily said as she started to clean up the mess.

Basil got up slowly and walked outside.

Now I've really made a mess of things! he thought as he headed for his favorite spot down by the stream. *I'm nothing but a big, clumsy bear!*

From farther down the bank, Basil heard friendly voices calling his name. It was the beaver family, Mr. and Mrs. Mudge and their baby. They were enjoying a picnic lunch and were taking a rest from building their new dam.

"Good day, Basil," said Mr. Mudge. "I'm sure you're looking forward to the pie-eating contest this afternoon."

"I *am*," said Basil as he bowed to say hello to Mrs. Mudge. "That's a fine-looking dam you're building."

"Now that you're here," said Mr. Mudge, "would you please help us with this log? It will be the finishing touch for our new home."

Basil was happy to help. He lifted the log and carried it to the edge of the bank. Just as he was about to place the log over the dam, his foot slipped in the mud and he fell headfirst into the stream with a loud SPLASH! Mr. and Mrs. Mudge dove into the water after Basil. As they helped him out, he saw the log floating downstream.

"That's alright, Basil," chuckled Mrs. Mudge. "We can get another log."

Basil climbed up the stream bank and said, "I'll see you at the fair this afternoon. Wish me luck at the pie-eating contest!"

"We'll be there to cheer for you," said Mrs. Mudge.

Holly the raccoon and her little kit, Chester, were busy hanging clothes out to dry in their backyard. Holly looked up from her work to see the sad sight of Basil walking toward her, his clothes still soggy.

"Dear, dear Basil . . . what's happened? Did you go for a swim with your clothes on?"

"Oh, no, Holly. I'm just a big, clumsy bear. I can't do anything right!"

"Try not to let it upset you, dear. Think of all the things you do well," Holly said.

Basil smiled. "Well, I *do* make the best raspberry tarts in all of Bywater Hollow," he said.

"Of course you do. And your applesauce cake is heavenly! Now hand me a clothespin, please."

Basil handed her a clothespin and gave little Chester a pat on his head.

"I'll see you both at the fair this afternoon," he said. But as he said this he accidentally backed into Holly's clothesline. The line broke, and all the clothes dropped to the ground. One of Chester's shirts fell over Basil's head. All he could say was "Mumpph!" Holly pulled the shirt off his head.

"A big, clumsy bear . . . that's all I am!" he said. Holly just shook her head.

Now it was mid-afternoon and Basil, more miserable than ever, wandered toward an open meadow. The blue sky was dotted with brightly colored kites. Nelson, Bywater Hollow's only flying squirrel, called to Basil.

"Oh, Basil, Basil! I need your help."

Basil saw that Nelson was having trouble launching his kite.

"Here, Basil, you hold the kite, and I'll jump on."

Basil ran out to the center of the meadow, pulling Nelson and the kite up into the air.

"We're a great kite-flying team, aren't we?" called Nelson from above a maple tree.

"The very best!" Basil called back. All of Basil's cares floated away as the kite climbed higher and higher. But suddenly the gentle breeze changed direction, and Basil could not keep the kite from landing right in the middle of the maple tree.

Nelson glided down to the ground and looked up at the damaged kite, caught in the highest branches of the old tree. "Oh, no! Basil, my kite! It's torn!" he said.

"I'll climb up and see if I can get it," said Basil. Slowly but surely Basil climbed the huge tree, but he could not reach the kite. He heard someone calling his name, not from below but from up in the sky.

"Look up, Basil, look up!"

There, floating above him, Basil saw Violet the skunk, Mr. Nidd the badger, and Grimsby Squill the porcupine in a beautiful hot-air balloon.

"Can we help?" called Grimsby as he guided the balloon to a hovering position over the tree. Basil grabbed the balloon's basket with one paw to steady himself and reached for the kite. His foot slipped, and the tree limb he was balanced on began to bend down.

"Oh, no!" said Basil. "I'm going to fall, I just know it!"

"Hold on to the basket, Basil!" cried Mr. Nidd. The hot-air
balloon rose quickly, and Basil managed to pull himself headfirst
into the basket.

"I can't do anything right," he said quietly. "I'm just a big, clumsy bear."

It was late afternoon when Grimsby slowly guided his balloon down to the fairgrounds. Everyone from far and near had come to the Bywater Hollow Fair.

Basil and his friends climbed out of the basket, and Violet looked up at him.

"I'm sure you'll win the pie-eating contest, but remember, Basil, even if you don't, you're still a good bear."

TICKETS

SIGN UP HERE
FOR
PIE-EATING
CONTEST

Basil smiled at Violet's kind words and tried to forget the unhappy events of the day. But he could not help feeling a little scared as he joined the crowd streaming into the pie–eating contest tent. He found his place at a table along with the other contestants. There were so many pies! Basil was so nervous he wasn't sure he could eat even one. Everyone in the tent crowded closer for a better view, but no one noticed that outside, dark clouds were drifting over the fairgrounds.

Grimsby Squill called for everyone's attention, then in a loud voice said, "Ready, set, BEGIN!"

Basil and the other contestants lost no time in gulping down
one pie after another as the crowd cheered them on.

Suddenly the tent flaps fluttered, then rose up and down as the wind started to blow. It blew harder and harder. Every animal in the tent became silent as they looked at each other in fear. Basil raised his head midway through his twelfth pie just in time to see the strong wind make the tent billow so high that its stakes were pulled up out of the ground. The main pole swayed, then fell, and the huge tent collapsed, covering everyone.